D1068372

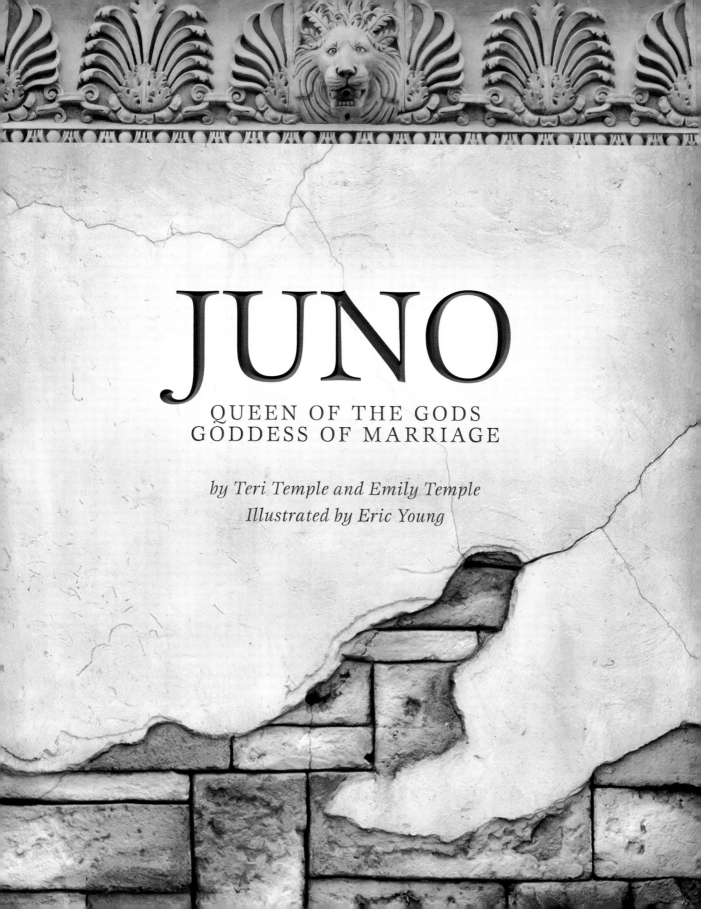

JUNO

QUEEN OF THE GODS
GODDESS OF MARRIAGE

by Teri Temple and Emily Temple
Illustrated by Eric Young

Published by The Child's World®
1980 Lookout Drive • Mankato, MN 56003-1705
800-599-READ • www.childsworld.com

ACKNOWLEDGMENTS
The Child's World®: Mary Berendes, Publishing Director
Red Line Editorial: Editorial direction
The Design Lab: Design and production
Design elements ©: Banana Republic Images/Shutterstock Images; Shutterstock
Images; Anton Balazh/Shutterstock Images
Photographs ©: Viacheslav Lopatin/Shutterstock Images, 5; North Wind
Picture Archives/AP Images, 10; Dorling Kindersley/Thinkstock, 15; iStock/
Thinkstock, 16; Peter Paul Rubens, 18; Solodov Alexey/Shutterstock Images,
20; Shutterstock Images, 22; Vahan Abrahamyan/Shutterstock Images, 27

ISBN 9781631437175
LCCN 2014945311

Printed in the United States of America
Mankato, MN
November, 2014
PA02241

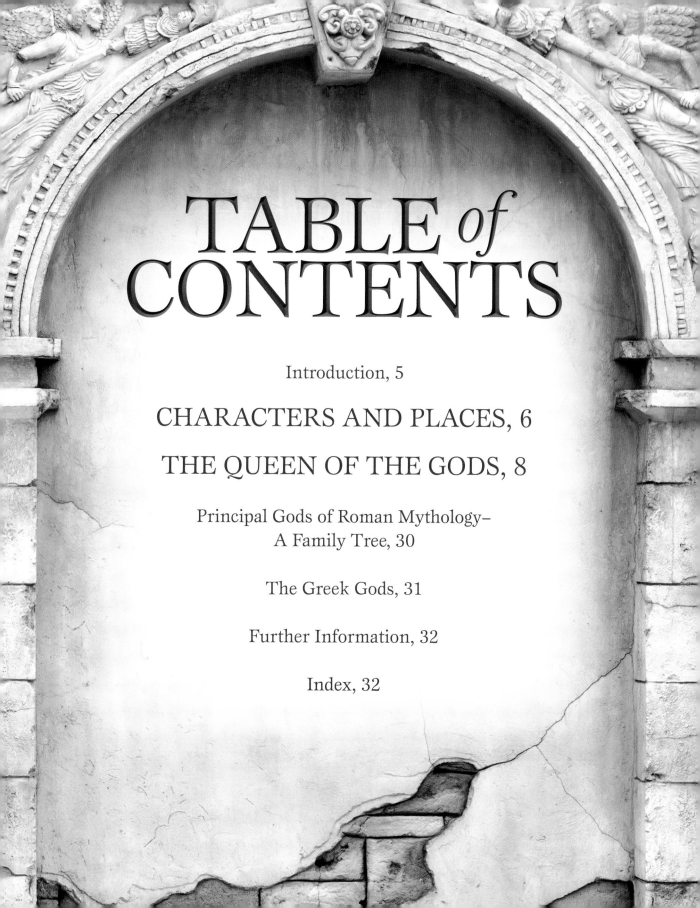

TABLE *of* CONTENTS

INTRODUCTION

In ancient times Romans believed in spirits or gods called numina. In Latin, *numina* means divine will or power. The Romans took part in religious rituals to please the gods. They felt the gods had powers that could make their lives better.

As the Roman government grew more powerful, its armies conquered many neighboring lands. Romans often adopted beliefs from these new cultures. They greatly admired the Greek arts and sciences. Gradually, the Romans combined the Greek myths and religion with their own. These stories shaped and influenced each part of a Roman citizen's daily life. Ancient Roman poets, such as Ovid and Virgil, wrote down these tales of wonder. Their writings became a part of Rome's great history. To the Romans, however, these stories were not just for entertainment. Roman mythology was their key to understanding the world.

ANCIENT ROMAN SOCIETIES
Ancient Roman society was divided into several groups. The patricians were the most powerful and wealthiest group. They often owned land and held power in the government. The plebeians worked for the patricians. Slaves were prisoners of war or children without parents. Some slaves were freed and enjoyed most of the rights of citizens.

CHARACTERS AND PLACES

ANCIENT ROME

N

W

S

ADRIATIC SEA

ROME

TYRRHENIAN SEA

CARTHAGE *(KAHR-thij)*: *An ancient city-state in North Africa, near modern Tunis; founded by the Phoenicians in the middle of the 9th century BC; destroyed in 146 BC in the last of the Punic Wars*

MOUNT OLYMPUS *(mount uh-lim-PUHs)*: *The mountaintop home of the Olympic gods*

TROJAN WAR: *War between the ancient Greeks and Trojans*

AENEAS *(ih-NEE-uhs)*

Hero of the Trojan War; son of Anchises and Venus; founder of Rome

ARGUS *(AHR-guhs)*

A monster with 100 eyes; Juno's servant

DIDO *(DAHY-doh)*

A queen of Carthage who killed herself when abandoned by Aeneas

HERCULES *(HUR-kyuh-leez)*

Son of Jupiter; hero of Greek myths

IO *(EE-oh)*

A maiden seduced by Jupiter; when Juno was about to discover them together, Jupiter turned her into a white cow

JUNO *(JOO-noh)*

Queen of the gods; married to Jupiter

JUPITER *(JOO-pi-ter)*

Supreme ruler of the heavens and of the gods on Mount Olympus; son of Saturn and Ops; married to Juno; father of many gods and heroes

NEPTUNE *(NEP-toon)*

God of the seas and storms; brother to Jupiter

OPS *(ops)*

A Titaness; married to her brother Saturn; mother to the first six Olympic gods: Jupiter, Neptune, Pluto, Juno, Vesta, and Ceres

SATURN *(SAT-ern)*

A Titan who ruled the world; married to Ops, their children became the first six Olympic gods

OLYMPIAN GODS

(uh-LIM-pee-uhn): Ceres with daughter Proserpine, Mercury, Vulcan, Venus with son Cupid, Mars, Juno, Jupiter, Neptune, Minerva, Apollo, Diana, Bacchus, Vesta, and Pluto

THE QUEEN OF
THE GODS

Of all the goddesses on Mount Olympus, Juno was the greatest. But her story was almost not told. Juno's parents were the mighty Titans, Saturn and Ops. When their children were born, Saturn swallowed each one. He was afraid of being overthrown by one of them. This made Ops sad.

Ops made a plan before their sixth child, Jupiter, was born. Ops hid him on the island of Crete. Then she gave Saturn a stone wrapped in a blanket. He swallowed it, thinking it was the last baby. Jupiter grew up on Crete. Then he came to Mount Olympus. He tricked Saturn into drinking a potion. This made Saturn throw up all of his children. Those included Neptune, Pluto, Vesta, Ceres, and Juno.

Jupiter led his siblings in battle against their father. It lasted ten years. Terra, or Mother Earth, wanted the fighting to stop. She decided to help Jupiter. Powerful creatures called Cyclopes and Hecatoncheires joined Jupiter's side. They helped Jupiter defeat Saturn.

Jupiter took over as supreme ruler. He divided the reign of the universe amongst his brothers. The gods built a magnificent palace high in the clouds called Mount Olympus. The gods and goddesses lived there and watched over the earth.

Following the battle, the Titans Oceanus and Tethys
helped raise Juno. Juno grew up to be a beautiful goddess.
It wasn't long before Jupiter took notice of her loveliness.
He thought Juno was his perfect match. They began
planning a marvelous wedding.

Jupiter asked his messenger, Mercury, to invite all the
gods, men, and animals. Juno arrived wearing a stunning
crown of diamonds. She rode in a chariot pulled by
peacocks. This was her sacred bird.
Jupiter and Juno threw a royal
party that everyone attended.
Terra gave Juno a beautiful
tree that grew golden apples.
Juno planted it in the Garden
of Hesperides. She left a giant
dragon named Argus to guard it.
Argus was a monster with 100
eyes. Juno and Jupiter went on a
honeymoon that lasted 300 years.

ANCIENT WEDDING CUSTOMS
In ancient Rome some marriages
were arranged. The bride's
family provided a dowry to
the groom's family. A dowry is
money or property given as a
gift. Some Romans exchanged
rings. A dinner and a party
normally followed the wedding.
The month of June is named after
Juno because it was the most
popular month to get married in.

Juno was now the queen of the gods. She was also the goddess of women, marriage, and childbirth. It was believed that Juno watched over all women from birth until death.

Juno is often compared to the Greek goddess Hera. Both goddesses were married to the king of the gods. This was often difficult. Jupiter and Zeus were known for their love affairs. Hera was described as a jealous wife. She wanted revenge on the women who caught her husband's attention.

However, Juno was seen as the graceful mother of Rome. Juno was first an independent Italian goddess. Romans prayed to her for successful marriages, pregnancies, and healthy children. Juno spent most of her time protecting women. She carried a scepter and commonly wore a veil on her head with lilies and roses in her hair. Juno had 14 nymphs as companions. Her most trusted was Iris, the goddess of the rainbow.

Jupiter and Juno ruled over Mount Olympus. They had three children. Their first son was Vulcan. He was born ugly and deformed. At first sight, Juno dropped Vulcan out of Olympus. Vulcan's legs were injured in the fall. He became the god of fire.

Juno's second son was Mars. Romans believed Juno had Mars without Jupiter. She was mad at her husband over the birth of his daughter Minerva. Legend says Juno took a magic herb to become pregnant. Mars was the violent god of war. He was so mean even Jupiter and Juno did not like him.

Jupiter and Juno also had a daughter, Juventas. She was the gentle goddess of youth. She served drinks on Mount Olympus.

Life for Jupiter and Juno should have been perfect and carefree, but it was not.

PATERFAMILIAS
Family was the most important thing to ancient Romans. The household included children, blood relatives, spouses, and slaves. The *paterfamilias* was the oldest male in the family. He was responsible for all the actions of the family. Paterfamilias had the power of life and death over the entire family, too. In some families, the father and mother educated the children. The family all lived together in one house.

Juno believed Jupiter spent a lot of time on Earth seeing other women. She was right. Juno sometimes got very upset. She would then bother these women and their children. Even though Jupiter was the most powerful god, he was afraid of his wife. As a result, Jupiter snuck out of the palace to visit the women he loved.

One woman was a river nymph named Io. Jupiter and Io had a secret hiding place. He hid this place with a thick, dark cloud. Juno saw through his plan. But right before Juno caught Jupiter and Io, the god turned Io into a white cow. Juno asked where the cow came from. Jupiter said it sprang from the earth. Pretending to believe him, Juno asked for the cow as a gift. She took Io to her Garden of Hesperides. Juno left the cow tied to her tree. It was

LETO AND THE TWINS

Another victim of Juno's anger was Leto. A Titan and goddess of motherhood, Leto married Jupiter. They soon found out she was pregnant with twins. Juno threw such a huge fit that Jupiter abandoned Leto. Chased by a giant serpent, Leto finally came to the island of Delos. There she was able to give birth to her twins, Apollo and Diana. They became the gods of the sun and the moon.

under the watchful eyes of Argus. He was a faithful servant to Juno. Poor Io was trapped as a cow.

Jupiter finally had enough of Juno's revenge. He sent Mercury to kill Argus. Mercury disguised himself as a shepherd. He walked by the monster playing enchanting music. Argus asked Mercury to sit with him. Then Argus asked Mercury about the panpipes he had been playing. He had never seen them before. Mercury began to tell him the story of their creation. Before long, all 100 of Argus's eyes were closed. Mercury tapped Argus with his wand and made him fall asleep. Then he used a mighty sword to cut off Argus's head. When Juno saw what Mercury had done, she took Argus's eyes and put them on the tail of her favorite bird, the peacock.

SEMELE

Semele was not as lucky as Io. She was the human mother of Bacchus. Jupiter loved Semele and promised to give her anything her heart desired. But he needed Semele to keep their relationship a secret. Unfortunately, Juno found out and began to plot her revenge. She tricked Semele into asking Jupiter to show his true form. Jupiter pleaded with Semele. He knew that any mortal who saw a god would die. But Jupiter had made a promise. When Jupiter revealed himself as a god, Semele was consumed by fire and died.

Then Jupiter promised to never set eyes on Io again. Juno agreed to let Jupiter return Io to her human form. Jupiter was not too upset. He had already moved on to his next love.

Jupiter's wives and lovers were not the only ones to feel Juno's rage. She often took out her frustration on his children as well. Juno did not like Hercules. As a baby, Hercules lived with his mother and stepfather. Juno was not happy with this arrangement. She sent snakes to his home to try to kill him. Hercules thought the snakes were toys and accidentally killed them.

As Hercules grew, he developed exceptional strength. He became a hero. Juno did not like that Hercules was respected. She made him go crazy. Hercules thought his children were someone else, and he killed them. Horrified by his actions, Hercules went to an oracle. An oracle was a special priest who offered advice on how to be forgiven. The oracle told Hercules he should complete ten labors.

THE NINTH LABOR OF HERCULES

One of the labors Juno picked for Hercules was to fetch the golden girdle that belonged to the queen of the Amazons. The Amazons were a race of female warriors. Juno thought they would stop Hercules. Instead, the queen, Hippolyte, offered to give him the girdle. Juno was angry. She disguised herself as an Amazon. Then she spread a rumor that Hercules was there to kidnap the queen. A battle broke out. The queen was killed in the scuffle. But Hercules got her golden girdle.

Hercules became a servant to King Eurystheus. Juno was overjoyed. She and the king worked together to come up with the hardest labors possible. Even when they added two extra labors, Hercules still acted bravely. The gods made him immortal and welcomed him back to Mount Olympus.

Juno's powers were great. Her stories of revenge filled the ancient Romans with awe. They worshiped her entirely. They witnessed what happened when she was angry, so they tried hard to keep her happy.

The Trojan War was one instance when it was a mistake to be on her bad side. It might have ended peacefully if not for Juno. The war began after a quarrel amongst the goddesses. A Trojan prince named Paris said Venus was the most beautiful goddess. Juno resented his decision. She set out to get even with him. The Trojans fought the Greeks for ten years. All of the gods took sides in the war. Juno, Minerva, and Neptune sided with the Greeks. The Trojans had Apollo, Diana, Venus, and Mars. Jupiter tried to stay neutral, but eventually chose to help Troy.

HOMER

Homer was a great poet in ancient Greece. He is believed to have written the poems *Iliad* and *Odyssey*. They told all the stories and heroic events of the Trojan War. Homer was a poet in the oral tradition. This meant that instead of writing the words down, he traveled from place to place and recited the stories. It was likely many years before they were finally written down. People all over the world still read them today.

Paris had fallen in love with Jupiter's daughter Helen. Juno went to Jupiter. Her beauty dazzled him. Juno was able to charm him to sleep. Without Jupiter, the war shifted. The Greeks snuck into the city in a great wooden horse. The Trojans thought it was a gift. Once inside the gates, the Greeks emerged and took over Troy.

Even after destroying the city of Troy, Juno was not happy. She turned her attention to Venus's son Aeneas. Aeneas was a native of Troy. He fled the city when it fell. The Trojans who survived joined Aeneas on a long journey to Italy. In search of a new home, they had to deal with Juno's wrath.

An ancient prophecy stated that a race descended from the Trojans would destroy the city of Carthage. Juno was angry because Carthage was her favorite city. Aeneas was headed for Italy. Juno thought the prophecy might be about him. She directed one of the gods of the winds, Aeolus, to bring a storm upon Aeneas. Just when Aeneas's fleet of ships seemed doomed, Neptune stepped in. Neptune told Aeolus to calm the waters. The seven remaining ships headed for the nearest land in sight. The violent storm had pushed them far off course. Now they were headed straight for Carthage.

Meanwhile, on Mount Olympus, Venus was concerned for her son. She pleaded with Jupiter to help Aeneas. Jupiter promised Aeneas would find his home in Italy. It was predicted that two of his descendants would start the mightiest empire in the world. Venus told Aeneas to go into the city. She told him a queen would welcome him with open arms. Queen Dido was excited to see such a famous hero. She invited Aeneas to have dinner with her at the palace. Aeneas told Dido all about his journey. He told her about the downfall of Troy. And he told her he was headed to Italy in search of the future he had been promised.

Still worried that Juno might interfere, Venus sent for Cupid, the god of love. Cupid made Queen Dido fall in love with Aeneas. Juno was pleased with this new development. She thought Aeneas would stay in Carthage forever with a queen who loved him. Unfortunately, she was wrong. The gods reminded Aeneas of his destiny, and he sailed away. Left alone, Dido was so distraught she killed herself. Juno was furious over the turn of events.

JASON AND THE ARGONAUTS
There are some stories in which Juno was the protector. The story of Jason and the Argonauts is an example. According to legend, a band of 50 heroes went with Jason in the ship *Argo*. They were going to fetch the Golden Fleece. This fleece would help Jason win a throne. Juno filled each Argonaut with the desire not be left behind and to always seek courage. Juno also helped Jason deal with the dangers the ship met along the way.

Juno was one of the most important goddesses in Roman mythology. Her worship was widespread during ancient times.

As part of worshiping Juno, ancient Romans held a feast day in her name each year on March 1. Married women had a procession to the temple. They prayed and made offerings to Juno. Their husbands would give them gifts. Juno was a guardian of women.

Juno was given many different names and titles. These represented the various roles she took on as a goddess. One of these names was Juno Moneta. Juno Moneta was the guardian of the finances of the empire. Romans built the Temple of Juno Moneta in 344 BC. This temple was located next to the Roman mint. The words "mint" and "money" come from the name Moneta.

Juno was also worshiped as the patron goddess of Rome and the Roman Empire. She was worshipped with Jupiter and Minerva. Juno was recognized as a strong goddess. She maintains an important role in Roman mythology.

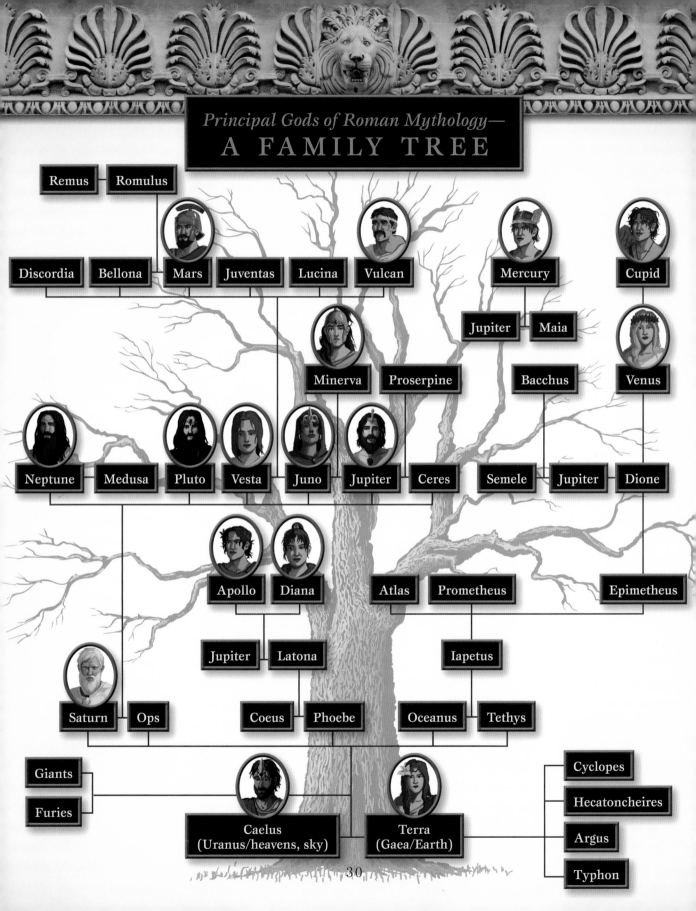

Principal Gods of Roman Mythology—
A FAMILY TREE

Remus — Romulus

Discordia — Bellona — Mars — Juventas — Lucina — Vulcan

Mercury

Cupid

Minerva — Proserpine

Jupiter — Maia

Bacchus

Venus

Neptune — Medusa — Pluto — Vesta — Juno — Jupiter — Ceres — Semele — Jupiter — Dione

Apollo — Diana

Atlas — Prometheus

Epimetheus

Jupiter — Latona

Iapetus

Saturn — Ops

Coeus — Phoebe

Oceanus — Tethys

Giants

Furies

Caelus
(Uranus/heavens, sky)

Terra
(Gaea/Earth)

Cyclopes

Hecatoncheires

Argus

Typhon

THE GREEK GODS

Ancient Greeks believed gods and goddesses ruled the world. The gods fell in love and struggled for power, but they never died. The ancient Greeks believed their gods were immortal. The Greek people worshiped the gods in temples. They felt the gods would protect and guide them. Over time, the Romans and many other cultures adopted the Greek myths as their own. While these other cultures changed the names of the gods, many of the stories remain the same.

SATURN: *Cronus*
God of Time and God of Sowing
Symbol: Sickle or Scythe

JUPITER: *Zeus*
King of the Gods, God of Sky, Rain, and Thunder
Symbols: Thunderbolt, Eagle, and Oak Tree

JUNO: *Hera*
Queen of the Gods, Goddess of Marriage,
*   Pregnancy, and Childbirth*
Symbols: Peacock, Cow, and Diadem
*   (Diamond Crown)*

NEPTUNE: *Poseidon*
God of the Sea
Symbols: Trident, Horse, and Dolphin

PLUTO: *Hades*
God of the Underworld
Symbols: Invisibility Helmet and Pomegranate

MINERVA: *Athena*
Goddess of Wisdom, War, and Arts and Crafts
Symbols: Owl, Shield, Loom, and Olive Tree

MARS: *Ares*
God of War
Symbols: Wild Boar, Vulture, and Dog

DIANA: *Artemis*
Goddess of the Moon and Hunt
Symbols: Deer, Moon, and Silver Bow and Arrows

APOLLO: *Apollo*
God of the Sun, Music, Healing, and Prophecy
Symbols: Laurel Tree, Lyre, Bow, and Raven

VENUS: *Aphrodite*
Goddess of Love and Beauty
Symbols: Dove, Swan, and Rose

CUPID: *Eros*
God of Love
Symbols: Bow and Arrows

MERCURY: *Hermes*
Messenger to the Gods, God of Travelers and Trade
Symbols: Crane, Caduceus, Winged Sandals,
*   and Helmet*

FURTHER INFORMATION

BOOKS

Johnson, Robin. *Understanding Roman Myths*. New York: Crabtree Publishing, 2012.

Temple, Teri. *Hera: Queen of the Gods, Goddess of Marriage*.
Mankato, MN: Child's World, 2013.

WEB SITES
Visit our Web site for links about Juno: *childsworld.com/links*

*Note to Parents, Teachers, and Librarians: We routinely verify our Web links to make sure
they are safe and active sites. So encourage your readers to check them out!*

INDEX